Paris Cat

Paris Cat LESLIE BAKER

LITTLE, BROWN AND COMPANY

Boston   New York   London

For David

If you are lucky to have lived in Paris as a young man,
then wherever you go for the rest of your life, it stays with you,
for Paris is a moveable feast.
— Ernest Hemingway

Copyright © 1999 by Leslie Baker

First Edition

Library of Congress Cataloging-in-Publication Data
Baker, Leslie A.
  Paris cat / Leslie Baker. — 1st ed.
    p.   cm.
  Summary: On their first day in Paris, Annie's cat goes off to chase a mouse and wanders around the
whole city before finding her way back where she belongs.
  ISBN 0-316-07309-1
  [1. Cats — Fiction. 2. Lost and found possessions — Fiction. 3. Paris (France) — Fiction.] I. Title.
PZ7.B1744Par 1999
[E] — dc21   97-42169

10 9 8 7 6 5 4 3 2 1

PC

Printed in the United States of America

The paintings for this book were done in watercolors on Arches paper.
The text was set in Adobe Garamond, and the display type is Bellevue.

On the first day of her first trip to Paris, Alice spots something interesting in Great-Auntie Isabella's garden. A mouse! Alice can't resist a good chase — or such a tasty treat.

As Great-Auntie Isabella is hugging Annie, Alice takes off. *"Mon Dieu!"* cries Auntie Isabella. "Your kitty is escaping!"

Annie runs after Alice, calling, "Alice, Alice, come back!" But Alice is having too much fun to listen.

She runs up one street and down another.
She zigzags through the crowds, getting closer and closer to the mouse but
farther and farther from Annie.

When Alice nearly collides with a man on a bicycle, the mouse dives to safety.
Her chase now over, Alice turns around to find her way back to Annie. But
she makes a wrong turn . . .

. . . and ends up in a crowded outdoor market. Her nose twitches with delight
at all the delicious smells

Mmmmm . . . cheese . . . sausages . . . fish. Mouse hunting has made Alice hungry. Where to begin?

Alice pauses beneath a fish stall, hoping for a taste. She waits patiently and is rewarded when a small fish slips from a customer's bag and flops in front of her.

Alice is about to take a bite when a tomcat hisses at her and claims the prize for himself. Alice hisses back, then turns and heads down the street.

Mon Dieu! Paris is full of dogs! Dogs strolling by the market stands. Dogs going in and out of shops. Dogs with fancy outfits. Alice even spots a dog eating from his own dish at a café.

It's time to find Annie, decides Alice. But first she must sneak by all those dogs.

Suddenly a small terrier spots her and begins to bark wildly. Alice hurries on, but the terrier chases her out of the market and through the streets.

As they pass some book stalls along the banks of the Seine, Alice begins to slow down. But the terrier gets closer and closer.

To escape, Alice joins a crowd entering the Louvre. She looks around carefully. No dogs here. Alice enjoys the peace and quiet inside the museum, taking time to admire the paintings.

But not for long. A museum guard catches sight of her and shouts, "No cats allowed!" Alice dashes for the door, more determined than ever to find Annie. Where can she be?

Halfway across a magnificent bridge, one of those pesky dogs blocks Alice's path. She leaps onto a ledge to escape, but the rude little fellow snaps at her. Alice's fur stands on end, and she slowly backs away.

Suddenly she slips! She tries to catch herself, but the dog lunges at her. Alice falls off the bridge to the Seine below...

. . . where she lands safely on the roof of a *bateau-mouche*. Alice travels up the river . . .

. . . and down again. Where is Annie?

When the boat docks, Alice jumps off in search of her. Which way to go?

Alice walks all over Paris looking for Annie, but nothing looks familiar to her.
She is lost.

Tired, thirsty, and very dirty, Alice strolls through a quiet park. She pauses before a flower bed. The petals look inviting.

Soon Alice is catnapping peacefully among them.

When the sun goes down on the Paris afternoon, Alice awakens to the shouts of a gardener waving a rake at her. A crowd has gathered around Alice — and in the crowd are Annie and Great-Auntie Isabella!

"Have you been sleeping here all this time, while I've been looking for you all over Paris?" Annie asks Alice.

Alice almost smiles.

E
BAK

Baker, Leslie A.

Paris cat.

$15.95 Grades 1-2 08/19/1999

DATE			

000069   149248